SPEAKEASY

Also by A. M. Dunnewin

The Benighted Saga

The Benighted

Speakeasy Novellas

Speakeasy

Rum Runner

SPEAKEASY

A NOVELLA

A. M. DUNNEWIN

Dark Hour
—PRESS—

First published in the United States of America by A. M. Dunnewin, 2011
Published by Dark Hour Press, LLC, 2016

Published by Dark Hour Press, LLC, California.

www.darkhourpress.com

Print ISBN: 978-0-9983929-8-1

Cover design by Dean Samed

Third Edition

To my loved ones.

CHAPTER ONE

. . . .

The cold New York air clung to the few pedestrians that walked the streets, the heavy thoughts of rain appearing in the way they wore their hats and coats, bundled underneath their clothing as the automobiles drove by them in a fast moving luxury. The night lights flashed against the backdrop of the buildings, glittering onto the wet streets, and the New Yorkers moved against the dark currents, the warm thoughts of the next best thing clustering in their minds and herding them to the next hot spot. Most were dressed in fine apparel while a few distant remnants of the working class moved among them.

On one of the countless streets stood one of the elaborate picture palaces, a movie theater decorated like an Italian mansion dubbed with rich greenery, velvet seating, and a twilight mural overhead that twinkled with electric bulbs. From the luxurious men's and women's lounges to the marble-lined hallways that mimicked cathedrals, under crystal chandeliers and up plush carpeted stairways, from nurseries to billiard rooms, all this was a part of the theater's scheme to flaunt lavishness. Able to seat over 4,500 people, its five stories of pure classical art was a phenomenon in itself.

There was, however, a very dark undertone in the theater's presence that only a few had the privilege of knowing. They would enter the theater like a regular movie patron, buying their tickets and lingering in the grand lobby as if waiting just like another well-dressed theater lover for their seats. But these fortunate comers would be waiting to see one of the special ushers, the handful of employees who knew of the secret hidden underneath the palace's foundation. Upon seeing him, they would recite a very precise saying which included a password, hidden in a conversation that only the usher's ears would pick up on. With a nod, the usher would depart in order to show the real movie-goers to their seats, and moments later would reappear with a nod as if it were their turn to be ushered into the theater.

They would pass the hallways, the elaborate arches and pillars, the walls that were draped in velvet curtains. They would steal a glance inside the picture palace's grand stage, hear the beginnings of the orchestra before the picture itself would start to play, catch a twinkling of the make-believe sky overhead. But as the lights dimmed and all attention was diverted to the screen, the usher would slightly move one of the curtains that covered the walls, and knock a certain way. A small peephole would open, another password produced, and then to their excitement a hidden door would quietly open. The usher would step aside, and they would be allowed to venture into a dark hallway lit by single bulbs that trailed down the middle of the ceiling.

Compared to the unknown abyss around them, following these bulbs would be like following a trail of stars, their minds set only on what was awaiting them. The hallway dipped down a flight of stairs, every step leading them closer to the faint sound of music, a trumpet throbbing in rhythm while they continued down the dim path. Finally, they would come to a door, and once opening it, the strangers would come face to face with the loud vibrations of jazz music, flappers, liquor pouring into crystal glasses, and a night filled with endless possibilities. They would hardly notice the decorative columns that held the underground heaven together, the blood red velvet drapes that were extended above the jazz band, or the way the lighting was positioned so only the dancers were illuminated, leaving the tables and booths along the sides to be wrapped in shadows.

With just the right password to the right usher, the speakeasy welcomed them all.

The year was 1925, and the night had started off like all the others. The flappers with their short bobs and sleek dresses were dancing and drinking endlessly with the men who either came with them or had just met, the crescendo of cheers and curses from the gambling tables, the haze from the cigarette and cigar smoke making the place seem dream-like, and the jazz band lighting the room on fire with their luminous beats. The place was filling up as the jazz band pumped music into the dancers, and the bar was continuously bustling with thirsty clientele. And like all the nights those last few months, standing there next to the bar was Eddie Durante, clad in his white dress shirt and charcoal gray trousers, his slick blonde hair combed back and glistening under the hazy lighting as he took a quick inventory of his bootlegged liquor.

"Because obviously," his friend commented as he approached, "your liquor seems to like to get up and walk away."

Eddie lightly shook his head, though keeping his gray eyes on the paper, his mind running over the list of liquors he needed to restock. "It runs when it hears the coppers coming."

His friend laughed, his tall frame matching Eddie's, but his humor much more light. "I don't blame 'em. Thank God ya have that secret door, or I would've created a new one in the wall."

"You could've used the trap door." Eddie subconsciously used his pencil to point to the area behind the bar where the door was located.

"And escape with the rest of these minions?" he laughed. "Being your friend should grant me *some* special privileges."

Eddie couldn't help but chuckle, though his gaze never departed from the paper. He didn't have to look at the man next to him to know that his dark hair was combed back to perfection, that his deep navy suit was clean and tailored, and that his sharp blue eyes were constantly scanning the speakeasy's natives, waiting to find his next love interest for the night. "So what brings you back, Anthony?" Eddie asked.

"What, ya think a little raid is gonna keep me away from this joint?" Anthony laughed at his own wit, turned to stare down a few choice flappers before looking back at Eddie. Looking his friend up and down, he realized Eddie was dressed down again, his sleeves rolled up a quarter-way and his jacket and tie nowhere in sight. He had only come to the speakeasy to work.

"Hey, ya need to live a little," Anthony interrupted, and when Eddie didn't respond, he reached over and plucked the pencil out of his hand. Eddie, with no interest to quarrel, simply leaned against the bar and looked at his friend, waiting for an explanation.

"Like I said," Anthony continued, his sharp blue eyes staring at him. "Ya need to live a little. Ya don't need to inventory every single night, raid or no raid."

"This is my business," Eddie reminded him.

"Yeah, and your welfare is my business. Ya haven't been the same," Anthony started, but then realized he had said too much.

Eddie stared him down, his gray eyes never wavering. "Since when?" he dared.

Anthony cleared his throat, unable to constrain his mouth. "Since your wife."

My wife, he thought. It had seemed like forever since someone had mentioned her. "What about her?" he managed to ask, though his voice could only rise just above a whisper.

Anthony fidgeted with the pencil in his hand before facing his friend. "She's gone, Eddie. And they paid for what they did to her. Ya need to start moving past it. Hell, it's been like four months—"

"Three months and sixteen days," Eddie mumbled, interrupting halfheartedly since the conversation did nothing for him.

"See?" Anthony pointed out. "That's not normal. Ya practically own a harem full of flappers here, and ya aren't even taking advantage of it."

"I don't want to take advantage of it," Eddie answered, finally grabbing the pencil back and settling himself back into his work.

Anthony watched in amazement, raising his hand to protest before slapping it down on the bar in defeat. "Fine," he replied. "Sorry I brought it up."

"It's not just the fact you brought it up," Eddie firmly answered, trying to keep his voice smooth despite the rough edge that was entering his tone. "We're not talking about some girl I picked up off the streets. We're talking about Kate, the girl

I married. Disrespecting her is disrespecting me."

"Till death do ya part?" Anthony mocked, his eyebrow rising in doubt.

The words caught in his throat, but Eddie was able to stumble through his friend's endless sarcasm. "As long as I live."

Anthony turned to the bartender, nodding his head that he wanted the usual, and the bartender poured a glass of gin and sat it down in front of him. Bringing the glass to his lips, Anthony added with a smirk, "I now pronounce ya clinically insane."

Eddie tried to ignore him by looking back down at his paper. He tried to remember where he had left off, but couldn't focus past the conversation Anthony had sparked. A tightness had grown in his chest and a pain behind his eyes, and he tried to breathe deeper in order to stay calm. He fought the instinct to feel sorry for himself, but not even the jazz music, the laughter and idle flirting of his patrons, or the clinking of glass as they cheered all around him to their remarkable lives could diverge Eddie from remembering. He could almost see again the black Model T as it was pulled out of the river, the bullet holes punctured up and down its side, the newspapers declaring one woman and two men dead—

"How can a woman say she has no rights when she wears a dress like that?" came a young, high-pitched voice from behind, derailing Eddie's thoughts before they could spiral again. "I'm practically losing my freedom just looking at her."

Eddie recognized that it was Marcus, the lanky kid whose inner shyness had been destroyed the moment he had succumbed to his first girlfriend. Anthony, of course, laughed along with Marcus's all-talk sexism, because despite his open approach to women, Marcus really had no idea what to do once he had one.

"Show me more skin, sweetheart, and I'll *give* up all my rights," Anthony yelled to the crowd, and Eddie could hear one flapper, the one they had aimed for, yell back, "Say something original!" Anthony had laughed until he heard her, and he was the only one left silent between Marcus and the giggling flappers who had overheard the exchange.

"You're just mad cause it's true," Marcus finally said after his own chuckling had died down, to which Anthony grumbled something into his glass.

Eddie, however, pretended like he wasn't there. He didn't want to participate in this bull session. He wanted to jump four months in the past, to be able to go home, to find Kate asleep in their bed. But his home was a ghost town now, and even the speakeasy had lost its sparkling glitz after that day he saw the bullet holes.

Marcus and Anthony's voices trailed into Eddie's ears, but he tried to ignore their chatter by looking the other way. He scanned the area to the left of him where booths hugged the far wall, wrapped in shadows so private parties or couples could enjoy the speakeasy without being noticed. He squinted a bit, and saw from the way the dark silhouettes were positioned that people were enjoying the seclusion right then, mainly gangsters, he could only assume.

Assume. Eddie tried not to laugh. He *knew* gangsters were over there, plotting things he had no interest in. He stared at one of the booths where bellowing cigar smoke escalated from the shadows, revealing that more than one person was seated there.

That's when he caught sight of the single trail of smoke coming from the corner. It was a faint trail of grayish white, protruding from the darkness in a slow, rolling manner. Eddie squinted a bit to see if he could make out a shadow or silhouette like he had already done, but was suddenly jolted from his activity when he felt a hand pat against his shoulder. "So guess what I've been doing?" Marcus interrupted.

"Yourself," Anthony quipped as he downed the rest of his gin.

"Besides that," Marcus answered indifferently before turning back to Eddie. "I was outside with that singer of yours. Caught her in the alleyway when I was coming in."

"I told you to stop coming in from the back door," Eddie warned.

Before Marcus could defend himself, Anthony questioned, "Back in the alleyway? She still comes in through there?"

"She's still with that guy," Eddie remarked, stealing another glance towards the corner. "And I won't have him stepping foot in this place until he can control his behavior."

Anthony shook his head but said nothing.

"So she actually talked to you this time?" Eddie continued, looking back at Marcus and his dark features, his black hair mimicking Anthony's style while his brown eyes revealed the innocence that was still festering inside him. He was a good kid with a good heart. It was just everything else about him that needed work.

"In more ways than one," Marcus mustered together.

"Let me guess," Anthony simpered as he signaled the bartender to refill his glass. "Instead of saying 'no,' she said 'hell no.'"

Anthony's infectious burst of laughter, and being able to picture that actually happening, caused Eddie to laugh with him, and despite it being directed at him, Marcus couldn't help the curves of a smile appearing on his face. "In more ways than one," was all he could say.

"This kid, I tell ya," Anthony couldn't stop laughing, even into his second glass. "He thinks he's a regular sheik in this joint, yet he can't even get that country girl singer to look at him."

"Don't underestimate country girls," Marcus spoke up, trying to get the bartender's attention that was now diverted to serving a group of flappers. "They're real bearcats."

Anthony shook his head at him, but decided to direct the conversation at Eddie. "So what about the country doll? If I wasn't mistaken, you two had a real thing for each other."

Eddie, who had tried to catch another glimpse at the corner and its scrolling smoke trail, finally rotated his body to meet his friends. Ignoring Anthony's comment, he went straight to Marcus. "Was Sal outside?"

Marcus finally flagged down the bartender, and once he told the bartender that he'd have the same as Anthony, he replied, "Yeah, just pulling up. Is he delivering tonight?"

"He better be," Eddie remarked, looking back over his list. "That raid did nothing for my stock. Thankfully they picked the night right before I was to be replenished."

"Excuse me," Anthony leaned forward a little, making his point by staring his friend down. "Don't pretend ya didn't hear me."

"I'm not pretending. I'm choosing not to."

Marcus sipped his drink, realizing that the gin Anthony was having only burned his throat. He made a sour face at it, but pulled himself together just long enough to enter the conversation. "You holding a torch for Lillian?"

Eddie stared from Marcus to Anthony. "No," he replied determinedly. "Lillian and I have a professional partnership.

That's all."

Anthony smiled a little. "But does she know that? Before what happened to Kate-"

"You're doing it again!" Eddie snapped.

"What? What am I doing?" Anthony questioned, throwing his hands in the air out of exasperation.

"Disrespecting," Eddie glared, which even caused Marcus to lean back a little to not be in the line of sight.

Anthony, whose voice was always on a louder level, raised his vocals even more as he looked up at the ceiling. "For heaven's sake! Kate, I'm sorry, God rest your soul, but I'm just trying to make him have a life!"

"I don't need one," Eddie answered in irritation. "I'm just fine."

"Yeah, that's what women say right before the claws come out," Anthony grumbled. But it was too late, because without another word, Eddie snatched the pencil and paper up in his hand and started his march across the dance floor.

Watching him leave, Marcus tried another sip of the gin but failed, and sat it down next to Anthony. "He's not getting over it, is he?" Marcus questioned softly.

Anthony shook his head, and downed the rest of his glass before taking up Marcus' leftovers. He turned to watch Eddie, noticed how his free hand was in his pocket now, how the young man walked among the dancers without a single thought to joining them. Eddie walked by them all as if they didn't even exist, eventually disappearing into the shadows against the far wall. "No," was all Anthony could say.

"He married Kate, Anthony. Can ya blame him?" Marcus questioned, ordering a different drink.

Anthony couldn't respond as the name alone conjured up an image of deep auburn hair, bright hazel eyes, and the dimples that pressed into her cheeks when she smiled. All he could do was smile sadly at the thought of her, and he used the rest of Marcus' gin to privately toast to the memory of the sweetheart he had always carried a torch for.

CHAPTER TWO

. . . .

When Eddie opened the back door and stepped out into the alleyway, he was met with the chilling night air and two black and tan Chrysler Six automobiles that were just starting to be unloaded by a small group of bootleggers. Eddie couldn't help but chuckle, remembering when the two cars had been purchased at the beginning of the previous year. They had been trophy cars, the first of their kind that his uncle just had to have. Now seeing the luxury vehicles being used for work made Eddie remember just how rich and materialistic his uncle was. *He's probably riding around in a '26 Rolls Royce, for all I know,* he thought.

"It's about to rain pitchforks out here!" one of the men growled, his way of telling the others to hurry up considering the rain hadn't started up again. His short, heavy stature remained in the middle of the commotion, glaring at the slowness of the men who were unloading his liquor.

"Well, maybe if you had enough money, you could buy the weather," Eddie joked as he approached, wishing he had grabbed his jacket before he had come outside.

"Ha!" the older man replied, smiling up at him. His face was rosy from the cold air, and the brown fedora he wore only made his own brown eyes look more shifty than usual. "I got enough money. He's just too stubborn to give it up."

Eddie smiled, though he couldn't bring himself to laugh. It took just too much effort, especially with the cold prickling through his shirt. "So how's life been treating you, Sal?"

Sal shrugged, keeping his eyes on the men who were unloading the liquor from the automobiles into the speakeasy's back door. "Still kicking," he remarked, and then noticed Eddie's trembling body. "Did ya lose your jacket? What you got there?"

Eddie, who had crossed his arms to preserve some warmth, looked at the pencil and paper he was still holding. "Just a quick inventory," he remarked absentmindedly.

Sal eyed him, but thought nothing of it as he looked down at his feet. "How's the rest of your joint? Those coppers didn't make too much of a mess, did they?"

Eddie shook his head, trying to hide the shivering that he could feel on his lips. "They didn't even find the door. One of my guys saw them go towards the curtain and prematurely flipped the switch. The moment everyone saw the red light, chaos broke out. But I have to admit, the back counter worked perfectly. They wouldn't have found one bottle."

Sal laughed at the irony. "Well, don't thank me, thank your uncle. He got the idea from being at 21 during a raid. A few levers pulled, shelves tipped back toward a chute and no bottles were seen again. No one would think to check the sewers."

"Well, it worked beautifully," Eddie commented, a little disheartened that he wasn't the first to have such a smart trick up his sleeve. "How is my uncle?"

"Hitting on all sixes, I'm told. He recently left for Italy, gone to visit the family."

Eddie nodded, but couldn't bring himself to say anything. He looked around at the other men, noticing that they weren't making eye-contact with him as they worked. Eddie, however, didn't have time to wonder about it. His teeth were beginning to chatter, and he was about to excuse himself when Sal turned to face him head on.

"There's something I'd like to discuss, if ya don't mind," he remarked, staring at him unwaveringly until Eddie complied and followed him to one of the automobiles. Rounding the car, Eddie opened the door and got in.

Once the doors were closed, Sal didn't take long to get right to the point. "They know it was you, Eddie."

The words slapped him across the face, but Eddie didn't respond.

"That you were the one who came up with the idea," Sal continued. "They're out for retaliation, and it's rumored that they've sent a torpedo into this juice joint of yours. That's part of the reason why I'm not being too open with the information. Afraid of who might be listening."

A hit man in his speakeasy. Eddie stared out the windshield, watching Sal begin to light a cigarette out of the corner of his eye. "I had a lot of ideas," he remarked hoarsely, fear and dread subtly mixing into his thoughts.

"Only took one," Sal responded as he lit the cigarette. He silently offered one to Eddie, who refused with a shake of his head. "Sorry, kid," Sal explained as he took a puff. "After what they did to your wife, I wouldn't have blamed ya."

Eddie remained silent, his eyes drifting to the bootleggers who were moving the last of the crates. No wonder they weren't laying their eyes on him. He was a dead target.

Sal took another drag on his cigarette, taking a moment for himself. "Don't worry, though," he finally remarked. "Your family's got your back. My brother-in-law, your dear uncle, has requested that Joe stay by your side until we can square away if there's a torpedo and who it is."

"What?" Eddie balked, shattering his calm exterior.

"It's temporary," Sal cooed, trying to calm the young man down. "He's just some extra protection."

Eddie gawked, unable to believe that they'd send Joe, of all people, to protect him. "He's crazy," was all Eddie could summarize when it came to his cousin.

"He's happy," Sal tried to smooth over.

"*Trigger* happy," Eddie corrected.

Sal shrugged his shoulders. "He gets the job done. And when the boss' favorite nephew needs protection, the boss will only send the very best."

"I don't need protection," Eddie fought back, trying not to raise his voice to the lunacy. "And even if I did, I have Anthony and Marcus in there—"

"Little orphan Anthony and Baby Marcus?" Sal choked, half laughing, half sputtering on the cigarette smoke. "Marcus is too naive, and Anthony," but Sal had to chuckle first before he could continue. "Well, ya better just pray your killer isn't a female."

"Thanks for warning me," Eddie begrudgingly admitted as he pulled the door handle.

"Just be careful, kid," Sal commented, and Eddie nodded in thanks.

When Eddie stepped out of the automobile, he suddenly came face to face with Joe. Joe's stained teeth, disheveled brown hair and unkempt black suit only added to the irksome character that was just waiting to come out. "So he told ya?" Joe asked, excitement pulsing through his veins.

Eddie took a deep breath, hearing Sal chuckling in the car behind him. "Yeah, he told me."

"Riveting, isn't it?"

Eddie rolled his eyes as he slammed the door shut. With the paper and pencil clutched tightly in his hand, he crossed his arms again as he trudged back over to the speakeasy's back entrance, Joe following on his heels.

"That idea ya had for the pizzeria was Jake," Joe continued, never wavering from the fulfillment he had experienced. "Ya must be so proud of the results. I mean, who wouldn't be? It was art in its finest form."

Eddie's eyes narrowed in disgust as he reached the door. "Yeah, I'm swimming in satisfaction," he remarked coldly.

"I don't blame ya," Joe smiled as he followed his cousin inside the building.

The two men walked down the flight of steps and through a dank hallway lit by a single row of lights that glowed overhead, passing a door on either side of them before coming to a door that marked the end of the hallway. They could hear the faint sounds of the jazz band, the gaiety of the people on the other side. Eddie grabbed the handle and turned it, unlatching the door. Pushing it open just enough to let themselves through one at a time, Eddie and Joe emerged against the dark backdrop of the shadows that hugged the walls of the speakeasy. The men's eyes were easily diverted to the lighted dance floor, the beads and sequins glistening off the dresses of the flappers as they danced with their gentlemen friends. Eddie pushed the door closed, instantly becoming flush with the wall as Joe continued to stare at the scene.

Once done, Eddie went and stood by his cousin, letting the man enjoy the surroundings. He equally looked at the wave of flappers as they glittered underneath the lights, some with feathers in their hair, but could only think of how his wife had never joined the fashion. She had kept her auburn hair long and wavy, her clothes modest yet feminine. She had defied the fashion craze that was taking over their generation, and he had never appreciated her for it as much as he did now, looking over the cliché sex appeal that every woman had seemed to mimic. Kate had always been one step ahead of them.

I need you to be here, he couldn't stop himself from thinking, trying to picture Kate among the flappers, her white blouse more attractive than any amount of sequins could muster up.

"Heaven never looked so good," Joe commented as he and Eddie crossed out of the shadows and onto the dance floor. The jazz was bursting around them, the colors moving together in spontaneous rhythm, the sexuality vibrating from the movement of the flappers and ricocheting off their dates. Joe slipped his hand through his disheveled and greasy hair, pointing his finger like a gun at a couple of the clientele, who saw it and quickly disappeared. With a little jig in his step that was offbeat and a wild craze in his eyes, Joe moved among the crowd with a spastic enjoyment, causing Eddie's lip to curl in repulsion.

The cousins moved passed the dancers, Joe unable to take everything in at once. "Check out the stilts on that doll," he'd comment, his eyes locked on a pair of legs, or "That baby vamp's got the goods," when an attractive woman caught his eye. Eddie tried not to listen as he directed them to where Marcus and Anthony were still standing by the bar. The closer they approached, Eddie could see that Anthony and Marcus were with a small group of flappers, Anthony paying close attention to one of them while the other girls glanced at each other and giggled, and Marcus slinking to the background, eager to participate but not knowing how to start. Eddie also began to hear the remnants of their conversation.

"Then how about ya show me this devotion of yours?" Anthony's love interest cooed, her shimmering blue dress somehow matching the piercing blue of his eyes.

"Cash or check?" Anthony replied, before looking at Marcus. "I love how it has a double meaning." With that, he laughed despite the disgusted look from his date after she realized what he meant.

"Oh, go chase yourself," Marcus mumbled, a little sore about not having one of the flappers hanging off of him. "Ya mock romance now, but back in the day, serenades and poems were the makings of heroic knights when they went off to battle. Their only correspondence was the paper to which they poured their heart on, their slang being the honesty which they sent to their loves."

The company could only stare in response, Anthony in bafflement while the flappers melted. "How romantic," one of them swooned, dreamy-eyed.

"It's history," Marcus tried to smile suavely, one of his eyebrows arched to act more rouge.

"Well, aren't ya full of information," Anthony mocked a compliment. However, wanting to snap the flappers out of believing the romantic crap Marcus had just conjured up, he barked, "Now go drain it!" He shoved the younger man away to initiate his point, but when he turned towards his date, he was met with her hand against his mouth. "Sorry, baby. The bank's closed." She and her friends walked away from him with a sly smirk and swaying rears, leaving Anthony with his hands wide open and his mouth dropped in shock.

Eddie tried not to laugh when he approached them, but Joe couldn't contain himself. "I thought you'd be used to rejection by now."

"Well, if it ain't Joe Durante in the flesh," Anthony mused with a smile, pulling himself together. "What the hell are *you* doing here?"

"Business," Joe answered, a knowing smile spreading across his face as he winked to Eddie before stepping up to the bar. Anthony laughed as he suavely approached Eddie, and in a harsh whisper, demanded, "Seriously, what the hell's he doing here?"

"It's complicated," Eddie began to say before seeing Joe turn around and ending his conversation.

"You're damn straight it's complicated," Joe laughed as he gulped his drink down before anyone had a chance to know what he had ordered. "Look at all these women! I've already committed apodyopsis so many times, it's terrifying even me."

"What do ya mean?" Anthony questioned back to Eddie, while Marcus remained stuck on Joe's use of wording.

"Is that even a real word?" Marcus asked with suspicion.

"Of course it is," Joe replied a little snootily. "Ya never heard of undressing people with your eyes?" Joe looked Marcus up and down, causing the younger man to take a step back. "By the looks of ya, I can see not," Joe continued, "It's an English word, kid. Look it up."

Before Marcus could protest, Anthony threw a hand up. "Excuse me, but I'm still back in the conversation that's wondering why you're here."

"For business reasons," Joe snubbed, his hand going through his hair again and somehow making it look more disheveled than sleek. The action caused Anthony to subconsciously check his own hair style to make sure it wasn't ending up like Joe's.

Realizing Joe wasn't going to elaborate, all eyes diverted to Eddie who tried to act nonchalant about it. "It's nothing. It's just Joe being Joe."

"Joe being Joe," his cousin sang as he winked at a distant flapper. Each of the men swore they heard the girl give a small shriek in disgust.

Eddie stepped closer to his cousin, trying to keep his voice calm and sincere despite wanting to beat him with a baseball bat. "Joe, why don't you go enjoy yourself. Go find yourself a nice girl and break her heart, okay?"

"No problem, Mr. Durante," Joe replied, his smile evidence that he agreed to follow orders.

The formality confused Eddie, especially coming from Joe. "Why are you calling me that?"

Joe looked around as if hoping no one was eavesdropping on what he was about to say. "It makes it more professional," he replied softly. "And a hit man's gotta have a professional demeanor in this day and age."

"I don't think professionalism really has anything to do with it," Marcus remarked, startling Joe who could have sworn that he had kept his voice low enough despite the men listening intently to him.

"Are *you* a hired gun? Do *you* get paid to take people out?"

Marcus shook his head like a little boy who was getting scolded.

"Exactly, so shut your face before I stick my dactylion where the sun don't shine."

"So *that's* what you've named it," Anthony mocked.

"You're just jealous cause you're not a part of a concilliabule like me."

"They used to hang people for that," Anthony smirked when Joe's eyes grew big.

Joe, despite the reaction, fell back into pretending that he didn't hear it as he straightened his dull black jacket out before bringing his attention back to the whole group. "If you'll excuse me, my duty awaits," and with that said, Joe sauntered away from the group, only turning back once to glare at Anthony.

"What's going on?" Anthony demanded.

"Yeah, why is a hit man in your joint?" Marcus pressed further.

Eddie could only shake his head, his eyes varying from his cousin to the smoke arising from the corner, coming from a booth with an occupant he was curious to see. However, turning back to his friends, he reassured them that nothing was wrong—as far as Joe was concerned. "He's just here as a favor to Sal. Let him have his fun."

"Well, no worries there," Anthony exclaimed, glaring at the gangster who had taken up with the flapper he had just spoken to moments ago, picking up where he had left off. Before Anthony could pick up his drink and start in, he concluded, "His fun and my fun are two separate countries."

Eddie, starting to feel the effects of being overwhelmed, tried to calm himself by diverting his attention elsewhere. His eyes automatically scanned the back shelf of the bar, noticing that the bar was running lower on resources than before. Setting his pencil and paper down since the list was now obsolete, Eddie announced, "I'm going to take a mental list of what's running low up here. Will you help me get some from the back when I'm done?"

Anthony, too busy downing the glass that he had neglected due to the flapper, only saluted him with his hand, which Eddie could only take as a yes. When he departed, Marcus decided to approach a bitter subject.

"So I understand why ya dislike Joe, but why so much?" he questioned, keeping his voice down so the jazz would drain out the conversation in case Eddie was in earshot.

Anthony slammed the glass on the counter, his way of congratulating himself for taking the shot. "Because he's a lunatic and he's a gangster, and I don't like the combination."

"So what, ya don't like the combination so you'll never trust the guy?" Marcus asked.

Anthony had to laugh at Marcus. Did he even hear himself? "Let me tell ya a little story," he said once he fought the last of his giggles. "Lillian's boyfriend was a regular here, came in every night to watch his sweetheart sing and to have a good time. So he's sitting over there near the band, kicking back with a couple drinks, when he notices someone watching her with that look in their eye, like they've known every part of her, if ya know what I mean.

"So Lillian's fella gets up and confronts him, because there's no mistake this guy's carrying a strong torch for his girl. They throw a few words back and forth until finally Lillian's boyfriend gets fed up and punches the guy. Moral of the story is that Lillian's boyfriend comes home to find a couple of men in his apartment who beat him until he's out cold. Lillian walks in on him bleeding all over the living room floor, rushes him to the hospital, and he spends the next three months recuperating. The reason why he drops her off in the alleyway isn't just because he's afraid to set foot in this place. It's because they disfigured his face, and he's ashamed of people seeing him. They gave him a total make-over all because he confronted a guy about having a crush on his doll."

"That's awful," Marcus responded, though sensing something else. "But what's the punch line?"

Anthony smiled knowingly. "The guy who'd been confronted was Eddie."

The younger man grew silent, remembering a day when Eddie had had a black eye, claiming a customer had been too rowdy. He had never thought to hear the whole story. Marcus watched Anthony order another drink, watched as his jaw slightly clenched, and felt he had to come to Eddie's defense. "Eddie wouldn't have set 'em up to it, though."

"No, but what's done is done." Anthony looked right at Marcus before adding, "That's why I don't trust *them*. His family acts like it never happened. Out there's a guy walking around with a face that doesn't even look like his own anymore, and the people who did it don't give two shits about him. Look at what happened to Kate. Over some pathetic territory dispute."

Marcus played with the glass that was still in his hand, but didn't bother to take a sip. "Well, you're his best friend," he commented, almost condemning Anthony.

"Yeah," Anthony smirked, seeing that Eddie was ready to head to the back rooms. Before turning to follow, he finished with, "Doesn't mean I gotta love *everything* about the guy."

CHAPTER THREE

. . . .

    Anthony trailed Eddie to the far wall, to the exact location where Eddie and Joe had entered through earlier. Up close, this part of the wall looked like all the others, decorative panels etched into it with holes and rivets outlining the designs. Taking out a long, thin key with a magnet attached to the end, Eddie pushed the key into one of the holes. The magnets locked together which in turn unlatched the secret door that was disguised in front of them. It was a three inch thick solid oak door, making it hard to find if someone knocked on it, thinking they'd hear a hollow sound.

    Crossing the threshold, Eddie placed the key back in his pocket as he grabbed the handle and pulled the door to a close, hearing it latch. Anthony followed Eddie down the lighted hallway, coming to a door on the right side which Eddie used as an office.

    "So ya gonna explain his presence?" Anthony finally spoke once they had entered the room, coming face to face with cases of liquor packed away in crates with fruit labels on them.

    Eddie started opening one of the crates. "Does it

matter?"

"Very," Anthony explained as he approached, stuffing his hands in his pockets. "A hit man in a speakeasy isn't exactly glamorous. I don't care what people think."

Eddie kept his mouth shut. He took a look around the room, trying to get his bearings as he tried to think of something to say that would put Anthony off for a while. The room wasn't very big with mainly a large safe in the corner and a desk that sat towards the right wall. The rest of the space was dedicated for the crates of extra liquor. It seemed to him that somehow the bootleggers had stashed more crates in the office than usual, for the stacks seemed taller — almost as tall as him — and broadened outward so that there was only a small trail that led to the desk and safe. Eddie only shrugged it off, figuring it was a small gift from Sal, probably a "sorry I had to tell ya that ya might be bumped off tonight" token.

"Hey, ya gotta leak over here," Anthony interrupted, and Eddie found that he was pointing to a crimson red liquid that was slowly oozing out from in between two of the crates. Anthony stepped closer, looking at it more clearly. "It can't be what I think it is, is it?"

Eddie stepped over, his heart thumping against his ribs, causing his body to tremble slightly. Squatting down, Eddie poked his finger into the substance, and then brought it up for a closer investigation. The crimson color smeared across his fingers, but it was when he smelled the familiar odor that he realized it was blood. He looked up at Anthony, solemnly nodding his head before standing back up. On full alert, Eddie began to move the crates away from where the blood was coming from. Anthony scrambled to help, and only after a couple of tall rows had been moved aside did they find the body behind it, blockaded and surrounded by the bootlegged bounty.

The two men stared at the body, at the five bullet holes that had burrowed into the back of his jacket, at the blood that had seeped out from underneath him. Eddie, revolted by the sight, couldn't help but see who it was, and when he did, he let out a slow curse.

"Who's that?" Anthony questioned.

"It's Frank," Eddie replied, dread in his tone. "My uncle's bodyguard."

Anthony looked around the room, looking at the open door and around the crevices of the crates. "So if his bodyguard's here, where's he?"

"In Italy," Eddie managed to say as he covered his mouth, swearing he could already smell death. "Sal said he was in Italy."

"And he just so happened to forget his bodyguard?" Anthony gawked, his own panic starting to make him edgy. "What the hell's going on?"

Eddie closed his eyes as he confessed, "Sal said there's a hit man in the speakeasy, and I'm his target."

Anthony's eyes grew a little wider, his concern evident from the shock on his face. All he could do was put his hands on his hips, taking in the situation as he stared at the body before him. After a long moment, he finally responded with, "Well, he missed."

Eddie shook his head as if trying to shake the scene out of his mind. "I'm going to check on Lillian," he said, his voice dry and the creases in his brow revealing how troubled he was. "Hide him behind the crates, will you?"

Anthony saw the anxiety, and with understanding, he nodded.

It didn't take Eddie long to escape the room, and before

he walked to the dressing room, he stood with his hand against the wall, steadying himself as he tried to breath. Blinking his eyes and trying to concentrate, Eddie continued moving down the hallway until he approached the entrance to the cleaning room that had half been converted into the dressing room.

The room itself was small, with a large vanity on the left wall, clothes racks that lined the right wall, and a large metal shelving unit used for storage on the back wall. The shelves were strong and packed full of miscellaneous things, causing more boxes and crates to flood the corners and making the room even more cramped. The three large trunks stacked in the corner didn't help much, either.

However, Eddie didn't get the clustered feeling he usually got. His eyes were immediately drawn to the red fringed gown, the sequins that sparkled like diamonds against her curves, the sequined headband with the luscious black feather that stood up from behind her short, curly blonde hair, done up in a finger wave hairstyle. He knew her face would be made up just right, her smoky brown eyes that held just enough seduction to turn heads, the full red lips that were made for kissing, and the golden ringlet that would rebelliously fall just over her right eye halfway through the night, making her a mystery to her audience. Despite her country roots, New York had gotten under her skin.

She was putting on her deep red lipstick, puckering her lips up in the reflection of the mirror. She was the epitome for sophisticated chic, a self-assurance in her movements that would carry her through the evening. "I'm almost ready," she called out, and Eddie realized she knew he was there.

"That's fine," Eddie answered. "I was just wondering if everything was ok in here."

"Of course it is," Lillian said with no feeling, too busy

fixing her lipstick.

Eddie tried hard to phrase his question without drawing too much attention. "You didn't by chance hear anything while you were in here? I had a delivery and wanted to make sure no one bothered you."

Lillian shrugged as she finished with her lips. "I haven't heard or seen anyone, except Marcus when he walked in with me."

"Your lips look redder than usual. It's nice." Eddie put his hands in his pant pockets, trying to act calm. The color looked oddly familiar, though he refused to bring the subject up.

Lillian, however, frowned as she replied, "I was hoping you wouldn't notice." She stood up, the look of resentment flowing into her actions.

Eddie felt she might as well slap him and get it over with, but he tried to play nice for his own nerves sake. "I'm sorry I admired it."

"It's not admiring that I have a problem with, Eddie. It's recognizing it." Lillian finally looked at him, but her usual sassiness had been replaced with almost guilt. "It's Kate's lipstick. She gave it to me about a week before—"

"Kate knew what she was doing by giving you that," Eddie interrupted, smiling proudly in hopes of stopping Lillian before she started. "She always thought you looked beautiful on stage, and sang beautifully." His words trailed off, and all he was left to do was look at the floor, feeling the emptiness thrash around in his body.

Lillian couldn't help but smile a little. "She was a sweetheart. I remember she'd always wish me good luck when she was here. Always made a point to see me before I went on stage."

Eddie had to turn away at that point. He kept his hands in his pockets as he stared at the opposite wall and the clothes racks, seeing nothing except Kate.

"I haven't told you," Lillian continued with awkwardness in her tone, "that I am really sorry for what happened. I read about it in the paper."

Eddie could see it then, the street corner that the car had been stopped at, and the bullet holes that riveted against the side of the Model T. The witnesses who were around had told the police that the gun firing seemed to have come out of nowhere.

"Of all the people, she didn't deserve to die that way," Lillian had continued.

"She wanted to see the parade that Macy's was putting on," Eddie softly replied, keeping his back to her. "I'd heard about the territory dispute between my family and the Caprice family. I asked Max and Eric if they could drive her there, look out for her since I had business to attend to here."

"It was a good thing you didn't see what happened. There's nothing romantic about watching someone die," Lillian answered, unable to contain her bitterness. Eddie knew why. She couldn't forgive him for what had happened to her, what she had found laying half dead in her living room.

"You would have to actually witness someone dying before coming to that conclusion," Eddie equally replied, his nerves too shot to keep tip-toeing around the subject

Lillian felt her temper slip. "I did, or did you just purposely forget? He might be alive, but a part of him died—"

"Did you really read what happened?" he demanded, angry that she had tried to parallel her beat-up boyfriend with his murdered wife.

Lillian batted her eyes, unable to speak as she watched

Eddie turn and glare at her.

"They were gunned down while stopped at a stop sign. Witnesses said my wife fell to the floor of the backseat while they fired, and when the gunmen were out of bullets, they said she leaned across the seat to grab the steering wheel, yelling for Max to put his foot on the gas despite being shot himself. When one of the gunmen saw her, he pulled out his gun at the last minute and shot her three times. But Max was somehow still alive enough to respond, and the car was seen swerving through the streets, my wife trying to steer a car with three bullet holes in her. They pursued her, Lillian, all the way to the docks."

Lillian stood frozen. She hadn't read all the details. "I shouldn't have brought it up—"

"It was hours later," Eddie recalled, not hearing her, "when I watched as they dragged that car out of the water, the right side lined with bullet holes. The windshield had been smashed through, and it was ruled by the detectives that she had been sent through the windshield when the car dove into the water." Eddie felt his throat tight up, but he couldn't stop. "They still can't find her. The police had the nerve to tell me that there's no chance she would have survived. If the bullet wounds or the windshield hadn't killed her, drowning would have. I checked every hospital around, every morgue, to see if somehow she had survived or was at least found, but there's nothing." A darkness clouded into Eddie's eyes that Lillian had never seen before. "But I'll tell you one thing, Lillian. She wasn't lying half dead on some living room floor, waiting to die. It's like she never existed."

"It hurts, doesn't it," Lillian hissed, her own darkness consuming her. "When someone you love is damaged beyond repair. Like they've never existed." She said the last words as if

Eddie had no idea what they actually meant.

Eddie smirked. "Damaged and destroyed are two very different things."

Lillian would have liked nothing more than to ram his words back down his throat from where they came. But she knew what had happened to her boyfriend was nothing compared to what had happened to his wife, and so she dropped her gaze, dropped the argument, and turned away to look at herself in the mirror, wondering why she hadn't left the speakeasy a long time ago.

Eddie looked away as well, staring at the clothes racks in front of him. He remembered the last time he had been in that room with Kate. He had been venting in the same spot about something ridiculous, and Kate only stood against the door frame, patiently listening to him. Her hair had fallen across one shoulder, her head tilted to the side as she watched him, and when he was done, he looked at her and found a simple expression. She was the only person he knew who could tell him so much just by looking at him. With understanding in her eyes, she had shaken her head at him, and he had folded under that gaze.

"If anything, there is one thing that needs to be made clear."

Eddie's eyes shifted back to Lillian, finding that her back was still toward him but that she was addressing him through the reflection in the mirror. He could see even from a distance that her soft brown eyes were moist. "Kate was never your weakness, Eddie. Your family is."

"Then leave," he simply retorted, walking over towards the metal shelving unit in order to get away from her mirror image. He put his left arm against one of the shelves, and rested his head on it, closing his eyes in hopes to escape everything around him. *I'm so sorry, baby*, he thought, envisioning her face watching him as she leaned against the door frame, her head still tilted to the side.

Then suddenly, as he tried to lose himself in thought, he felt a hand on his right shoulder. Not bothering to lift his head, he rolled his head to the side in order to see Lillian standing next to him, leaning against the shelves. "I'm so sorry," she confessed, her eyes watering even more.

Eddie couldn't help but step backward, away from her and everything she had stood for. But she followed him, raising her head to keep her eyes fixed on his. It was a passion they knew they wouldn't be able to resist or escape.

Their faces were just inches away, and he could practically taste her lips. When he closed his eyes, he was met with the image of a different girl peering up at him. She was laying on her stomach with her body twisted with the white linen sheets of their bed, her auburn hair cascading down her bare back, her shimmering hazel eyes were looking up at him, her skin creased from her smile. For a moment, Eddie felt relief.

And then, as instantly as the joy came, it faded when he opened his eyes and saw Lillian. Saw the smoky eyes and the golden ringlets, the deep red lips and the eager temptation in her brown eyes. He grimaced when he realized that she was never really what he wanted.

Lillian saw the expression, the emotion diminishing with each passing second. There was no lying to herself that she felt disappointed and a little more irritated at him, but nothing overtook her emotions like the humiliation she felt for having put herself in that situation. She backed away from him in order to gain space, but instead backed right into the metal shelves, hitting it with enough force to cause the structure to shake a little, and a couple boxes near the back to fall over onto the floor.

Eddie caught sight of the boxes, and then the bloody arm dangling over the side of one of the shelves. "Oh, shit!" he exhaled before realizing what he had said.

"What? Did I break something?" Her concern caused her to turn around, but she was disrupted halfway when Eddie grabbed both her shoulders and spun her towards him. "No, of course not, everything's great, why don't we get you on stage," he exploded with false enthusiasm as he put his arm around her and dragged her from the spot.

"But it's not time yet," she managed to say, yanking herself free from him. "I still have to finish getting ready."

Eddie quickly moved in front of her, hoping that he could divert her by keeping her back to the shelving unit. "You look fine how you are—"

"Are you that ashamed?" she demanded, her pride taking a bigger blow than she realized.

Eddie swallowed the knot that had formed in his throat, knowing that whichever way this conversation was going, it wasn't going to go well.

To his rescue walked in Anthony, who took in the scene between Eddie and Lillian. Then his eyes fell on the arm that dangled from the metal shelf behind them. "Oh my God, another one?" he exclaimed, unable to control himself.

Eddie turned around, his eyes large and his jaw clenched as he stared at his friend, who could only stand there dumbfounded. Anthony, too, couldn't believe it had escaped his mouth.

"Another what?" Lillian slightly demanded, feeling herself lose it.

Anthony stuttered, the shock of seeing another dead body unnerving him. "Ah…I ah…another angel has fallen from heaven." He shrugged his shoulders dramatically, speaking with his hands in an attempt to somehow make his rambling speech seem that much more believable. "Your beauty is unearthly, Lillian, and I can't stop myself from marveling at it."

"Are you kidding me?" Lillian spat.

"You caught me, I'm a natural poet."

Eddie stared at him, cocking his eyebrow as he covered his mouth with his fist, trying to keep himself under control, but he couldn't stop his eyes from shifting to Lillian, to see if she had somehow bought it.

Finally, after putting her hands on her hips and taking a deep breath, she shook her head at Eddie's friend. "Drinking too much already, Anthony?"

"Believe me, it hasn't been enough."

"I say it's been plenty," she resolved, walking past the men and back to the vanity.

"What the hell," Anthony mouthed to Eddie, shock and anger wrestling themselves to take over his facial expression. Eddie shook his head violently in order to shut Anthony up, though keeping his fist over his mouth out of apprehension.

"I swear, you fellas drive me up the wall sometimes. And when I ask, I get nothing. Well, fine. Play that game, but don't play it on my time. Now you two need to leave so I can finish getting ready." Before the men could react, Lillian had turned around to stare at them, and from where she stood, she had a direct line of vision to what Eddie had been trying to conceal. It only took a second for her eyes to widen as she realized what was hanging from the back shelf, dripping with crimson that was pooling on the floor.

"It's not entirely what you think—" Eddie tried to explain before Lillian screamed.

CHAPTER FOUR

. . . .

What happened next would later be a blur. Lillian, whose screams had surprisingly not shattered the vanity mirror, had tried to flee the dressing room but was caught halfway to the door by Eddie, already sensing she would try to run. He bear-hugged her, keeping her back to his chest as she tried to fling herself out of his grip, kicking her legs out and screaming as loud as she could. She moved so violently against him that Eddie was surprised he could even hang on. She shoved him back into the vanity, wheeled him in circles as she tried with all her might to break free from him, but he only moved with her, dancing against her fighting instincts and howling screams.

They didn't see Anthony standing there, more interested in the dead body that had been shoved in between the shelves than the duo that were wreaking havoc. So when Lillian decided to give it all she got, squeezing her eyes shut, jumping up and down, kicking her legs in order to fight Eddie, she didn't realize until she heard a man shriek that she had kicked Anthony straight in the groin.

Eddie and Lillian instantly froze. They watched as

Anthony dropped to his knees, holding himself before rolling onto his back, screaming and cursing as he went. Eddie let go of Lillian who ran to Anthony's side, standing over him as she cried in sympathy, "Oh, Anthony, I'm so sorry!"

"Why the jewels!" he screamed up at her. "Why the family jewels!"

"I'm sorry!" she shrieked back, her tone somehow louder than his.

Anthony could only cover his face with one hand, crying, "You heartless bitch!"

"I said I was sorry!" she yelled again, now irritated that she was apologizing to a grown man crying on the floor.

Eddie approached the two as they yelled at each other, and in a calm voice he didn't even know he could have, looked straight down at Anthony. "Are you going to be ok?"

Anthony, trying to hide the tears that were sparkling in his eyes, grunted, "Eventually."

Eddie nodded in response, but couldn't stop his gaze from shifting to the bloody arm. His first instinct was to leave the speakeasy all together, but pride wouldn't allow it, which left him with one choice. He slowly walked towards the shelving unit, saw how the body had been lifted and stuffed between the shelves, how the head was turned away from him in silent hopelessness. The body was once a big man, tall and burly and full of pride, Eddie could only imagine. It reminded him of his uncle, a man who would keep a tight hold on superiority despite the deceased overtone. Eddie looked down at the sleeve, seeing that the fabric was new, perfectly tailored to fit him.

Eddie felt his gut twist when his curiosity overcame him. He poked at the body, making sure the man was dead and nothing was going to grab him. Feeling somewhat relieved and somewhat silly, Eddie used his hand to pivot the face towards him. And when he did, he jumped back and covered his mouth with his hand, trying to somehow keep his stomach from climbing up his throat.

"Who is it?" Anthony called out from the floor. Lillian remained where she was, too scared to say anything.

Eddie felt the sweat on his brow, his mouth growing dry as he slowly removed his hand. "It's my uncle."

When Anthony heard the words, he slowly sat up on his elbows, the pain being replaced with cold tension. "That's not possible," he thought out loud, but was silenced when Eddie nodded his head.

Standing up as best as he could, Anthony shuffled over to Eddie and the body. When he saw the face, the chubby fat cheeks and the lifeless gray eyes, Anthony's own pulse started twitching. Although he couldn't stand straight very well, it didn't stop Anthony from locking eyes with his friend. "Now we know why the hit man's after ya. He's already killed everyone else."

"A hit man's after you?" Lillian panted, her voice quivering as she watched Eddie, who couldn't keep from looking back at his uncle.

"Makes ya just wanna cuddle with him, don't it?" Anthony interrupted, taking out his silver cigarette case and pulling a cigarette from it. His hands shook as he tried to proceed.

"Are you really going to light one up in here?" Eddie finally spoke, his nerves forcing him to take control of something. He was too irritated and terrified, too overwhelmed to realize what he was demanding, but he had to somehow construct order out of chaos. Besides, he had enjoyed having at least one room in the speakeasy that wasn't clouded over in some kind of smoke.

However, Eddie wasn't met with a full-hearted apology, or even a recoiled action. Instead, he was met with an ugly glare. Anthony, with his blue eyes bulging and his lips pressed together in a grim line, could only respond by pointing to his crotch. He had taken one for his friend, and by God he was going to have his cigarette. Eddie took a deep breath, and moved past the issue.

"What do you mean a hit man's after you?" Lillian shouted, beyond upset and pressing into hysterical.

"It doesn't really matter at this point," Eddie mumbled, crossing his arms and trying to take multiple deep breaths. How were they going to keep people from knowing? Where would they hide the bodies?

After finally getting a cigarette out, Anthony held it in the corner of his mouth. While fishing for a light, he said in a muffled tone, "Easy for *you* to say. We don't know who else is on this prelude list. How many appetizers are they gonna take out before they hit the main course?"

"There's no need to start becoming hysterical," Eddie replied, lowering his eyes at Lillian, who shot him an equally disturbed look.

After Anthony lit his cigarette, he looked at his friend in disbelief. "Oh, I'm sorry, Mr. My-uncle's-lying-dead-ten-inches-from-my-face. Apparently, me and Lil are the only ones spooked about all this."

"Like I'm not?" Eddie broke. "Dead bodies are popping up in my speakeasy and you think I'm not spooked? My name was supposed to be on top of the list!"

"There are more?" Lillian asked breathlessly, feeling faint while the men ignored her.

"Then why aren't *you* dead!" Anthony barked, yanking

the cigarette from his mouth. "They killed your uncle, Eddie. The boss! Nobody ever gets close to a boss like that. Ever!" Anthony paused just long enough to take a long drag from his cigarette. Blowing the smoke out, he continued as if he'd never stopped. "There's more to this than we know. I mean, how the hell did they get to him? Or his bodyguard? And why bring 'em here? They were obviously killed somewhere else, or there would be blood all over this joint."

"Panicking isn't going to get us anywhere." Eddie checked on Lillian who was trying to stay on her feet, lightly sweeping the fresh tears from her eyes, unable to hide the terror. "We'll keep the bodies where they are so people won't see. We don't need that kind of alarm or publicity. Not until we can figure this out."

"Then what do we do now?" Lillian spoke, her soft voice barely audible.

The men exchanged looks and Eddie finally answered, "I need to find Joe. Since these guys are here, I'll need a backup gunman when shit hits the fan."

"It's already hit the fan," Anthony balked, glancing at the bloody sleeve and the red pool of blood underneath it. "It's literally leaking all over the floor."

Lillian grimaced as she shook her head and turned away, unable to look anymore.

"Let's get out of here," Eddie resolved, walking towards the door. Lillian followed with Anthony trailing behind, all eager to leave death behind them.

They escaped out of the dressing room and down the hall until they met the back of the secret door. Walking over the hidden threshold, the three stepped foot into the heart of the speakeasy, the surreal scene looking the same as it always did. Yet there was something different, due to the anticipation that ran like ice water in their veins. All three subconsciously felt eyes watching them from the dark shadows. Instead of charging through the dance floor like Eddie and Joe had recently done, they slinked along the borders, teetering between shadow and light, walking a fine line between the known and the unknown.

They spotted Marcus at the bar by himself, ordering another drink from the bartender. He turned just as they approached, his eyes catching Lillian and a smile replacing his bored exterior. But then he saw the stone expressions and the absence of the bootlegged liquor.

"Where's Joe?" Eddie asked before Marcus could speak.

"I don't know. Last I saw he was with that flapper. I haven't seen him since."

"Neither have we," Eddie replied, his eyes turning to scan the dance floor. There was no sign of Joe. The flapper he and Anthony had both tangled with was laughing at a table where people were gambling, and the jazz music was hotter than ever, making the room pulsate with energy. Everyone around them was having a good time, and while Eddie continued to jump from one blissful, intoxicated face to the next, he again caught sight of the trail of cigarette smoke from the corner.

"I don't like this," he could hear Anthony grumble as Lillian grabbed a hold of Eddie's arm. Eddie turned to find her staring at him, worry filling her brown eyes.

"I'm going to go check the tables against the far wall," Eddie told her, and then addressed to the rest of the group, "He couldn't have gotten far."

Anthony nodded as he placed his hands in his pockets, Marcus gulped his drink down so he could be a part of the action, and Lillian refused to let go of Eddie's arm. With a grimace, Eddie turned and started back where they came, Lillian marching next to him as Anthony and Marcus followed.

They retraced their footsteps, coming back to the hidden door. From there, the men separated to search for Joe, leaving Eddie and Lillian alone together. The two walked along in silence until Eddie heard the crowd applaud and realized the band was changing songs. Taking in Lillian's glittering red dress and black feather ensemble, he suggested, "Why don't you go grab yourself a drink and head on stage. People are going to get curious why the singer is hanging around the owner instead of with the band."

Lillian responded with a tight grip on his arm. "After what I just witnessed, you really think I'll be able to sing normally?"

So much for getting rid of her, Eddie thought, a little uncomfortable that she was standing so close to him after the temptation they had endured earlier. And her nails digging into his arm didn't help either. The only way he could respond was by holding his tongue and searching for Joe, though Lillian made sure to hold on to his arm the entire time. They walked a few paces before Eddie noticed Anthony at a table to the distant right of where the band was playing, standing over a man whose body was slumped over the table top with almost eight empty glasses surrounding him.

As they made their way over, Eddie watched Anthony poke at the body, shaking his head at the drunk who was passed out. Grabbing a chunk of the guy's hair, Anthony pulled the head up, but immediately let go, causing the head to thud against the table top. Eddie quickened his steps, forcing Lillian to trot next to him.

Approaching the table, Eddie threw Lillian's hand off of his arm before going straight to Anthony, whose look of shock

41

only escalated his own alarm. "What's the problem?" he questioned.

Suddenly, they heard footsteps behind them, and when both men turned, they found Marcus shrugging his shoulders. "I didn't see him."

"That's because he's right here," Anthony answered, pointing down at the passed out man.

"Wow," Marcus remarked, taking a look over Joe whose face was planted into the wood. "How did he get so tanked up in such a short amount of time?" He motioned to the empty glasses, assuming the gangster was more intoxicated than normal.

"The real question's who drained him," Anthony replied as he seized Joe's hair and yanked his head up again. They were met not only with Joe's lifeless face, his eyes and mouth barely hanging open, but with a large slash from one side of his neck to the other. Upon seeing the blood, open muscle and exposed bone, it was evident that the only thing keeping Joe's head on his shoulders was the back flap of skin and muscle that hadn't been cut off. By the way the men jumped back at seeing the grotesque sight, and Lillian covering her mouth to shield her screams, Anthony let go of Joe's hair, allowing his head to fall back onto the table top, another thud escalating from where the head landed.

No explanations could be made, no comments addressed. Joe had been murdered in a room full of people, not one of them witnessing the event. There wasn't even evidence of Joe knowing that he was about to be murdered. Someone had simply come up behind him and cut his throat, and the jazz music had played on while the dancing and gambling had continued unfazed.

Eddie rubbed his hand through his thick hair, trying to

keep himself calm despite the trembling that was taking over his hands. While his gaze never left the body, he placed his hands on his hips while he addressed the group quietly. "We need to get him out of here. We can't have people see him. It would be a stampede in here if they knew."

"And bad for business," Marcus chirped in.

Eddie ignored the comment, too plagued with anxiety to think about how his business was going to survive after this. "Anthony," he instructed, "help me pick him up and we'll haul him into the dressing room."

"Why me," Anthony fired back. "He isn't my cousin!"

"Just do it," Eddie snapped, pushing Joe's body up so he sat straight up in the chair. Trying not to get too much blood on his fingers, Eddie undid Joe's tie and then wrapped it around the wound to stop the left over oozing, tying it with the remaining ends. Putting one of Joe's arms around his neck, Eddie looked up at Anthony who remained standing a distance away. Answering his look with an irritated sigh, Anthony reluctantly walked over and mimicked Eddie, resting Joe's arm on his shoulders.

"Oh man, did this guy ever bathe?" Anthony complained, being met with a sharp "shut up!" from Eddie as they heaved Joe out of the chair.

Crab walking him away from the table and chair, they started off slowly, Lillian and Marcus walking behind since they didn't know how to help. The small group was halfway to where the door was located when a stumbling drunk ran into Anthony, shoving the men to the side and causing Eddie to hit the wall. The action sandwiched Joe's body, to which both men tried to move away but were pulled back to their spots since Joe's arms were still around their necks. Lillian and Marcus froze in their tracks right behind them, unsure of how to react.

"Sorry there," the drunk slurred merrily. "I'd say I'm not the only one having a bad day." Eddie and Anthony's gaze followed to where the man was pointing, and found he was addressing Joe.

"He just had too much to drink," Eddie tried to explain, slightly smiling as if this situation wasn't new.

The man took one look at Joe's body, and concluded, "He looks dead to me."

No one could reply to him.

However, it was the drunken man who broke the short-lived silence just as cheerfully as he had started it. "But it ain't my problem." With that, he strolled away with a ringing laughter, disappearing among the dancers.

They watched him leave until Anthony turned to Eddie and said, "You need more clients like him."

Eddie glared as he fished around in his pocket for the magnetic key. Upon finding it, he stuck the magnet end in the hole and unlatched the door. As quickly as they could, the four living people and the dead body shuffled through the doorway, and the door was closed behind them, camouflaging back into the wall.

CHAPTER FIVE

. . . .

"So what's going on? Why's this all happening?" Marcus fired off.

"That's the question of the day," Anthony mumbled as he and Eddie laid Joe's body on the floor of the dressing room, next to the puddle of blood from Eddie's dead uncle.

Eddie took a deep breath, leaning against the shelves for support. *I wish you were here, baby*, he felt himself beg. *If you were here, we wouldn't be in this situation.*

"Might as well say something," Lillian softly taunted from behind them, her arms crossed in a meek fashion. She was trying so hard to stay brave despite the fear that lurked in every action.

"Sal explained to me tonight," Eddie finally managed to say, "that a hit man was placed in this joint, me being his target. He was sent by the Caprices."

Lillian's eyes grew wide as Marcus couldn't help but ask, "Why you?"

"They know that I was the one who came up with the idea."

Marcus looked at him in disbelief, taking a moment to compose himself. "You're talking about the pizzeria incident, aren't ya?"

Eddie nodded, and Marcus couldn't say another word.

"Pizzeria incident?" Lillian spoke up.

"Ya probably read about it," Anthony chimed in from where he stood. "It was titled the Massacre at The Old Pizzaiolo. Four of the biggest capos in the Caprice family who owned the restaurant were gunned down while eating dinner. It was known that they had money stashed there, in process of being transported to their boss, along with a stockpile of new guns and fine liquor."

"The three major food groups," Eddie added, though left the rest for Anthony to explain.

"Five men entered the pizzeria and opened fire with Tommy Guns without any warning."

"They killed everybody?" Lillian whispered, having a hard time comprehending what she was hearing.

"Let's just say there's a reason why those guns are nicknamed Chicago Typewriters," Anthony smiled knowingly. "They dictated that place to pieces. To my knowledge, they lost count of how many bullet holes were in the bodies. The men were shredded, and one of 'em couldn't even be identified by his face cause it had been shot up so badly. When the coppers finally arrived, the five men along with the three stashes were gone."

Lillian's mouth hung open until her eyes fell on Eddie. "That was your idea?"

Eddie slowly nodded. "It was retaliation for murdering my wife."

Lillian couldn't take her eyes off Eddie. "How could you?"

He tried to open his mouth to speak, but Marcus interrupted by saying directly to the singer, "Stop acting so surprised. Ya would've wanted him to react that way if *you* had been killed."

There was a bitterness in his tone that no one missed, and all Lillian could do was close her mouth. The silence that followed was deafening, and only Anthony could bring himself to speak.

"Listen, we need to get outta here. There's no point staying."

Eddie shook his head, while Marcus added, "What about the other people? Everyone here's in danger."

"We can stage a raid," Anthony considered. "I'll go up to the theater, turn the red light on, and when everyone sees, they'll scatter."

"Along with the hit man," Eddie counteracted, not liking the idea. "We'd draw too much attention to ourselves, and it would give the hit man a reason to leave and come back. There would be no end to it."

Anthony looked his friend straight in the eye. "There's only one end, and it's a final one. This guy's coming in and out as he pleases already, so might as well save some lives before they become part of the body count."

Eddie shook his head, but didn't say anything.

"But it would draw too much attention," Lillian spoke up from where she stood. "People would start asking questions when they found out there wasn't a raid. The police might try and get involved. There are too many open-ended questions. Besides, he's only harming people related to Eddie."

"Then *we* need to leave. Just us," Marcus suggested. "Get as far away from this joint as possible."

Anthony clapped his hands together, a smile brewing

on his face. "Now someone's on the trolley," he commented. "We'll go out the back door, find a ride and drive as fast as we can."

"I can't just run away from something like this," Eddie finally replied, dead set against leaving his speakeasy. "It wouldn't end."

"You'll run, even if I have to tie ya down to the hood of the car," Anthony replied as he and Marcus ushered Eddie out of the dressing room, down the hallway and up the stairs with Lillian in pursuit. "We'll find a set of wheels and get ourselves out of Dodge," Anthony explained as they reached the door.

"What about you," Eddie turned and asked Lillian, who was standing behind with her arms crossed again, a worried expression on her face.

"I'm a better singer than a runner," she commented softly.

Eddie looked her over, unable to help himself from imagining what could have been. He heard Anthony push the door open, and then out of the corner of his eye he saw Marcus suddenly lunge forward and grab Anthony's arm.

"Are ya insane?" Marcus hissed. "There could be people waiting outside. We need to check the surroundings first."

Eddie, surprised by the sudden reasoning, followed Anthony's gaze as they looked out the door, noticing that the two Chrysler Sixes were still parked right outside.

"Good luck," came a soft whisper, and Eddie turned slightly to find Lillian approaching him. With a small smile, he wrapped his arm around her in a half hug, telling her goodbye.

"Wait, where are the guys?" Anthony announced as Eddie looked back, realizing that no one was with the automobiles. "Did they go inside?"

Eddie looked from Anthony to the two cars, something

creeping up into the back of his mind. "I didn't see them," he replied, his arm still around Lillian whose eyes equally searched the scene.

"See?" Marcus asked in panic. "They're probably dead! And we're dead just standing here!"

"Ya need to relax," Anthony reminded him harshly, stealing a gaze at Lillian, and then Eddie. "There's no sense jumping to conclusions."

"They wouldn't have left the cars," Eddie thought out loud, Lillian shuddering against him. He looked over and found Marcus holding his head as he paced back and forth, whining to himself.

"There could be a reasonable exp—" Anthony started, but was cut off by the sound of a monstrous crash.

Everyone jumped and then stood frozen as they stared at the Chrysler Six that had been struck, its roof caved in by the impact. It only took a moment for them to see the legs and an arm to realize it was a body.

Lillian screamed, but was muffled out when Eddie pushed her face into his shoulder to keep her quiet. Marcus gasped as he held his head, his eyes wide in fear. Anthony began to take a step out of the doorway to investigate who it was when another body hit the ground to the right of the car, the body landing hard against the ground, sounding like a sack of flour as the head was smashed inward from the impact. Almost as fast as it had landed, blood began to seep from all around, forecasting that the fall had killed him.

Anthony let out a shallow curse as Marcus now held his hands over his mouth, trying not to scream like Lillian. Eddie kept Lillian's gaze away from the scene by holding her, but he couldn't take his own eyes away when he realized it was Sal who was lying on the pavement. "It's the bootleggers," Eddie whispered.

"His mouth," Anthony pointed out, all eyes except Lillian's now seeing that tape was covering Sal's mouth, silencing any scream before he hit the ground. Looking from one body to the other, Anthony curiously poked his head out and looked straight up against the building's wall and past the open stairwells until he could see the edge of the roof. "Oh my God," he suddenly gasped. "They're pushing 'em off the building."

As quickly as he had said it, Anthony suddenly shoved everyone back inside before another body was heard hitting the pavement to the left of them. Slamming the door, Anthony leaned back against it, trying to calm down from the adrenaline that was beating in his heart. "These guys are *not* messing around."

Eddie continued to hold Lillian, her cries never stopping. "Let's go back to the dressing room."

The others stared at him. "We can't just leave 'em like that," Marcus tried to explain.

"Marcus," Eddie tried to start, but couldn't bring himself to finalize that the men outside were dead and nothing could be done. The words wouldn't come to him. All he could do was shake his head as his young friend looked at him, a hopeful and naïve expression glazing over his eyes.

"If we go out there, we're dead," Anthony confirmed, stepping away from the door.

"But we can't leave 'em," Marcus persisted, unable to shake the guilt of watching someone die. "Some of 'em might still be alive."

"By all means," Anthony responded roughly as he opened the door to reveal the dark and bloody scene before them. "Go take a stroll down memory lane, and let us know what ya find."

"I don't need your sarcasm!" Marcus screamed, a terrible fear haunting him.

"And I don't need your ignorance," he counteracted, slamming the door. "Use your brain! Men being pushed off buildings isn't code for 'minor injury.' Those guys are dead, and so will we be if we go out there. Ya think the ones doing this aren't packing heat? You don't think they'll try to shoot us on the spot? They have the perfect angle on us." Anthony pointed to the ceiling, expanding on his idea.

Marcus glared back, but said nothing. The point had been clearly made.

"Let's get back to the dressing room," Eddie restated, already turning Lillian away and heading down the stairs. By the sound of thick heels clicking on the steps, Eddie knew the two other men were following.

Once in the dressing room, Eddie led Lillian to the vanity stool, sitting her down before searching the drawers for a spare handkerchief. To his relief, one was stuffed in the back of the bottom drawer, and he handed it to Lillian to help her recover. She thanked him by smiling sadly at him, and he stood watching her wipe parts of the eye make-up that had started to run before diverting his attention to the two bodies that were still against the back wall. Absentmindedly, Eddie ambled over to them, remembering the last conversation he had had with both. He hadn't spoken to his uncle for almost four months; Joe had been maybe an hour. He realized as he stood over their bodies that he really had never liked either of them. It had been a quest to know them personally, a quest he wished he had never taken.

Seeing some newspaper off to the side of him, Eddie grabbed one of the issues, opened it up and placed it over Joe's face, tired of looking at the man. Joe looked almost asleep, except for the blood-soaked tie that was still wrapped around his neck, and the drying blood that had poured down his shirt when his throat was cut. Eddie shook the disgust out of his head.

"Why did they kill them," sniffled Lillian, breaking the silence first.

"They're flexing their muscles," Eddie observed, looking from his cousin to his uncle. "Showing that if they can kill the boss, his bodyguard and his best gunman, I'm an easy target."

"So why the bootleggers?" Anthony piped up, and Eddie pivoted around to find that he was standing in the doorway, while Marcus stood across the room from Lillian, the uneasiness in him making him keep his distance from the group.

Eddie answered simply, "They're in the family."

Anthony shook his head even while Eddie spoke. "Ya know that can't be the real reason. The boss, his bodyguard, five other men. They aren't just flexing their muscles. Everyone who died was involved, weren't they?"

Eddie didn't want to respond. He didn't have to respond.

"Come on, Eddie," Anthony continued. "You aren't that stupid, and neither are we. The bootleggers and Joe were the gunmen, weren't they? Your uncle knew since he would have put the hit out, and of course his bodyguard would have known."

Eddie swallowed hard.

"And whatever happened to those things that were confiscated from The Old Pizzaiolo, huh? The bag of money, the guns, the liquor? A speakeasy like this would be an ideal place to hide it."

Eddie's eyes dropped to the floor, refusing to look at his friend for fear of losing his temper, despite heat crawling up the back of his neck.

"So they're taking everyone out," Marcus spoke up, still trying to understand the gist of what was happening. "But why say there's a hit on Eddie if they're just gonna kill everyone?"

"Because I came up with the idea," Eddie replied hoarsely, unable to control himself.

Anthony retorted. "Apparently, that doesn't matter too much since you're still standing here."

Eddie couldn't take it anymore. He couldn't dance around the subject pretending like it never happened. "The hit they put out on me isn't just for the pizzeria incident," Eddie snapped, his anxiety rising with his voice. "It's for the idea I put into action on November 27th of last year."

"November 27th? But that's the day that…" Anthony couldn't finish his sentence. His eyes grew wide as the realization slapped him across the face. "Ya couldn't have," was all he could mouth, though the words seemed to only be audible to Eddie, whose look of fault told him enough.

"It's when Macy's put on that parade. The uh," Marcus snapped his fingers until he remembered. "The Macy's Christmas Parade. We all went to go see it."

"Not all of us," Anthony whispered, darkness shadowing his eyes as he stared at Eddie.

Marcus looked from Anthony to Eddie until finally he remembered the other event that had occurred that day.

Eddie looked at each face and each ranging expression, from Anthony's that was in between shock and betrayal, to Lillian who was equally anxious in wanting clarification. Eddie addressed no one in particular when he spoke next, but only addressed to the room in hopes that he would be liberated by telling the truth. "The Caprices didn't kill my wife," he said. "We did."

CHAPTER SIX

. . . .

"It was going to turn into a territory war," Eddie started, his anxiety over the hit man being replaced by the tension in his audience. "The Caprices had been gaining territory close to my uncle's neighborhoods since the beginning of last year, and rumors were circulating that they were going to try and take over territory in my uncle's district. Everyone was at a standstill, the Caprices gaining just enough to piss off my uncle, while my uncle couldn't counterattack because they had yet to actually take some of his territory.

"However, my uncle didn't want to wait for them. He didn't want to lose or sacrifice anything. He wanted to hit them before they could strike, to show them not to mess with the Durantes before anything was gained or lost. But attacking a family for no reason would give the Caprices the advantage to gain allies against my uncle, and what ally would back up an instigator? My uncle would lose all the way around."

"Get to the point," Anthony growled, his head lowered but his eyes stabbing Eddie.

"My family wasn't too keen about me marrying Kate.

She had some Irish in her blood that they didn't like. I was already looked down on since my father had done the exact same thing, except with a mixed-blooded American. I was simply following in his footsteps.

"I've always wanted to belong with them though. Let me run this speakeasy, I begged them. I busted my ass for this place, and despite marrying Kate, they only kept me on because I was good at it.

"Back in October, I overheard a conversation Sal was having with one of the associates about the territory war. I spent the entire night thinking about it, wishing there was something I could do to prove that I was a part of this family. Just one chance to show that I belonged, not just as a relative who ran a speakeasy, but as a beloved nephew who belonged in the family business. A family who would always have my back. I had wanted that ever since I was a kid.

"So a couple of nights later, I approached Sal about an idea I had. Stage an attack, I said. Why not make the Caprices look like they attacked us, so when we gunned them down, no questions would be asked. In fact, allies would be flocking to us, and we could gain some territory in the process. Let's run 'em out of New York, I told him. Sal ate it up. Before I knew it, I was sitting with my uncle and getting a big pat on the back over it, being called his favorite nephew. But then he amended my idea. Why not stage a cold-blooded murder? The more drastic the scene, the harder we could counterattack. They just needed a victim. Someone close to the family but not too close to be of any significance.

"They wanted Kate," Eddie shook his head, hoping that the others didn't hear the crack in his voice. "They made it so I didn't have a choice but to agree."

"Choice?" Lillian broke in, her voice slightly shrieking.

"You didn't have a choice? You had plenty of them!"

"Dealing with gangsters, ya don't," Eddie replied, feeling exhausted. "I love Kate, but one thing was made clear in that room: blood comes first. So I told 'em I'd do it myself. If someone was going to kill my wife, it might as well be me since I started it. That's why I made the arrangements. I planned on November 27th, planned on her to be chauffeured in a car to see the parade, planned what street corner would work out perfectly. We needed witnesses, but not too many to be able to identify us. Just enough to give the coppers information that would point to the Caprice family.

"So on that morning, I told Kate that I wouldn't be able to make it to the parade because I had work to do here. I had planned on two associates to take her since they had wanted to go as well. I confessed to the territory war, and she took it as me being an overprotective husband. She left our apartment thinking that I was looking out for her.

"I was already gone by the time she left, but I didn't come to the speakeasy. The three bootleggers and I met at a bakery on the corner of the street I had set up. A Caprice car had been stolen, so dressed like Caprice members with those long heavy jackets and tilted fedoras, we got out and stood in front of the bakery as if we were admiring the food inside. We each had a Tommy Gun concealed in our jackets, and a black scarf around our necks to cover our faces in case we needed to hide our identity if someone got too close. One of the guys stayed behind the wheel.

"I was the one who saw the car first. They pulled up at the stop sign, and I signaled the driver to block 'em. He did what I said, but that bastard was too excited. He braked and jumped out before the car could block even half the front of the other car. So before Max could think of pulling away, we quickly covered our faces and opened fired on 'em. I saw my wife fall to the floor, and I remember how mangled Eric was when we finally stopped. I was sure by how many bullets we had put into the car that Kate didn't have a chance. It only took a few seconds.

"And then she sat up." At this point, Eddie had to take a breath, had to fight back the bewilderment he had felt that day when Kate looked right at him, recognizing him by the way he stood, by his eyes. The recognition on her face was all it took for her to lean across the driver's seat and for Eddie to bend down and grab the little handgun he kept hidden around his ankle and under his sock.

"She was screaming at him to put his foot on the gas. I managed to see a bullet had grazed his neck and she was putting pressure on it with her hand while she grabbed the wheel. I pointed the pistol at her and fired. I know three of the bullets hit her. Blood was everywhere at that point.

"Max was somehow still alive though, and I watched as the car shot forward, the tires screaming against the pavement from the jolt, the crash as her car slammed the tail-end of ours and shoved it out of the way. I ran after her, screaming at her to stop, my heart breaking against my ribs, watching as that car sped all over the road. I ran until another car came up beside me, and I found it was the three bootleggers in the stolen Caprice car. I jumped in and we followed after her, keeping our faces covered so the pedestrians on the street couldn't identify us. We trailed 'em to the docks. Max must have died shortly before they reached the river because the car never braked. We watched as the Model T drove straight off the pier and nose-dived into the Hudson. There was nothing we could do; we just watched as the last of the car sank."

Eddie looked at the faces around him, each one grim

and unable to speak. Since no one could say anything, Eddie decided to finish the story. "Afterwards, they got rid of the stolen car, while I was left to make my way back here. A couple hours later a paid detective of my uncle's found me and told me my wife had been killed. My plan had worked out perfectly. The stolen car had been found in the Caprice territory. The witnesses hadn't seen enough to identify us individually, but only as a group. Members of the Caprice family, they said. The detective found where the car had last been seen, and they were able to fish it out of the Hudson. I purposely watched, seeing if she survived. But when I saw the hole in the windshield, parts of her dress stuck in the glass, I knew just as well that she hadn't. The detective confirmed it by the witness testimonies. Kate Durante had been shot, chased to the docks, and was thrown out of the windshield. If she had survived the gunshots, the impact from the windshield alone would have knocked her unconscious and she would have drowned, not to mention the freezing temperatures of the river would have been against her."

"And ya say it like it's a good thing," Anthony finally responded, growling under his breath.

"For me," Eddie replied. "It was."

"How could ya, Eddie," Marcus cried out. "She was your wife! How could ya kill her for 'em?"

"Cause it's family," he answered, too matter-of-factly, even for himself.

"That means nothing," Anthony replied fiercely, starting to pace like a wild animal in a cage, his eyes never leaving Eddie. "Ya gunned down your own wife just so ya could belong to some piece of shit organization that's obsessed with blood. Ya were just trying to save your own skin."

"They put me behind the eight ball, alright? I had no

choice but to go along," Eddie shot back in defense. "Ya don't know what they would have done to me. Ya wouldn't understand—"

There was no warning when Anthony stormed toward him, grabbing Eddie by his throat and holding him just inches from his face. Seething through his teeth, Anthony yelled, "You're right, Durante! I *don't* understand! I don't understand how a little shit like *you* could even perceive an idea like that. I bet ya didn't even have the guts to tell 'em no when they said her name. This little idea ya have about family isn't normal. This isn't family, Eddie! This is a cult, and ya just played into their games!" By that point, Anthony couldn't even grip Eddie's throat tight enough, and with a shove, he released Eddie and took a step back to gain space from him. Eddie coughed until the air came back to his lungs.

"Ya don't even know what family is," Eddie defended, rubbing his throat as he addressed Anthony alone. "Ya can't even lay eyes on the same girl twice without fleeing to the next best thing. Ya have no sense of responsibility, no sense of duty. Blood's thicker than water, but little orphan Anthony wouldn't know a thing about that."

"And apparently *you* do," his friend fired back, his chest rising and falling with his hard breathing as his hands began to tremble in fury. "Ya murdered Kate just to appease your relatives so ya could be a part of the family. Well how does it feel, Eddie? How does it feel to be a part of the family now!"

Eddie watched as Anthony addressed his uncle's body, the blood that was drying and the remembrance of a hit man who was after him. "Ya don't understand what went on in that room!" Eddie screamed at his friend, his face red and his eyes watering. He didn't have anything else at that point, only the hope in his relatives.

"I loved her!" Anthony yelled before lowering his voice, unhappy with revealing the information. But looking at Eddie, seeing what was really in front of him, Anthony couldn't help but add, "It seems I was the only one who did."

That alone stopped Eddie in mid-thought. He hadn't realized the truth until he heard it, like a light being shined on an object he had subconsciously known was there but never thought about.

"Where's the stash?" Marcus softly asked, breaking into the tension.

Eddie wiped the cold sweat that had formed on his brow. "The liquor they took was what was on the shelf before the false raid. The guns are in the top trunk over there, I made sure this morning." He pointed to the corner where three large trunks were stacked. "And the money is in a safe place."

Anthony shook his head as he looked up at the ceiling. "My God, ya really did do all this," he mumbled.

"What can I say, Anthony," Eddie spat as he walked towards the trunks. "I'm an overachiever."

"You're certainly something," Anthony smiled as he looked back at Eddie, though there was a mean flame flickering in his eyes.

Eddie ignored him as he approached the trunks. A heaviness ached against his rib cage, but he tried to ignore it as he unlatched the top trunk and threw the lid open. What he was met with made him cringe, his mouth slowly dropping open at the scene before him. Eddie took a step back, unable to steady himself.

"They're gone, aren't they," he heard Anthony question, and he could only nod, unable to fully admit to the disappearance.

Marcus walked up to the trunk and peered in, his own

sense of wonder overcoming his anger. "But if these guys already have the guns, then why are they still here?" he asked, looking from Eddie to Anthony.

Eddie felt too dizzy to respond, and he had to close his eyes to block out the scene just so he could recapture some of his sanity.

While he meditated, it was Anthony who answered the question. "Because this was never about the stash. This was never about guns, or liquor, or even money. This is about revenge." Anthony put his hands in his pockets, a calm exterior while his insides felt hot with betrayal. "We were all dead the moment we stepped into this joint."

Eddie would have retorted, except a different sound broke into the conversation, the sound of heels echoing from the hallway, running up a flight of stairs. When the men looked over to where Lillian had been standing, they found she was gone.

Marcus cursed under his breath as he ran after her, and Anthony and Eddie had a brief stare down before they followed Marcus, chasing after him towards the stairwell and then to the door that led outside. They watched as Marcus broke through the door first, and once Anthony and Eddie reached the door, they were both halfway out into the drizzling rain when sputter gunshots filled the air. Marcus, upon reaching the Chrysler Six that hadn't been affected by the falling bootleggers, shook as the rapid bullets punctured his body, spraying blood everywhere. He convulsed until he fell lifeless to the ground, and Lillian, who had barricaded herself in the car, could only scream as she gripped the steering wheel, unable to look away from the kid whose crush on her had never gone unnoticed.

Hearing the gunshots come from overhead and seeing

Marcus go down, Anthony and Eddie both shoved themselves back into the doorway, peering out into the alleyway at Lillian who screamed and cried in the automobile, and the now five dead bodies whose blood were spreading against the wet ground.

"Get outta here, Lillian!" Anthony yelled at her, using his arms to gesture to her, trying to grab her attention.

"We don't know what they could've done to the car," Eddie warned, but was answered with a shove into the wall.

"This isn't your family we're dealing with," Anthony snapped at him before turning his attention back to the terrified singer. "Ya have to get outta here!" he yelled at her again, seeing that this time she was finally watching him.

"I can't," she whined into her tears, shaking her head.

"Lillian, sweetheart, ya have a chance to save yourself! Do it!" Anthony yelled back.

Then Eddie saw that she was staring at him through the rain, barely seeing her cheeks streaked with black, her smoky eyes draining with her tears. They looked at each other, the tension never wavering, the feelings still present. But Anthony was right. She had to save herself, and Eddie could see that she wanted to save herself from him.

The two men watched as she nodded, her golden ringlet bouncing over her eye as she agreed to leave. She found that the key was already in the ignition, and as she turned it, to her and the men's relief the engine roared to life. Then, without warning, the automobile exploded from inside out, a fireball explosion that sent a flash which temporarily blinded the men. The furious heat pushed against them as bits of debris blasted in all directions, and when they could finally peel their eyes open, all that was left was fire and metal. Through the whole incident, Eddie had heard a terrible scream, and it wasn't until

Anthony grabbed him and pulled him inside the building, that he realized it was himself.

Despite being inside, Eddie could still see the flashing inferno in front of him, still see her face before the car exploded. Eddie didn't know exactly when Anthony had released him, but when he came back to the present, he found he was against the wall at the base of the stairs, sliding down to the floor. He held his head in his hands all the way down, cursing under his breath, yelling when he couldn't speak. He pounded his fists into his forehead, grabbed at his hair, did everything self-destructive he could in order to overcome the internal pain. If he could, he would have clawed his way into his chest and ripped out his own heart so he could stop feeling. It took a few minutes for him to calm down enough to wipe the free-falling tears away and look up at Anthony, who was leaning against the wall across him. His hand covered his mouth, his own pain evident in the lines that creased his eyes as he tried to physically shut out the scene he had witnessed.

"I didn't mean for any of this," Eddie whispered, though it came out as a hiss from the way he choked on the air, how his body refused everything to help him overcome his pains. "He was just a kid. They both were just kids. They didn't deserve that."

Anthony didn't move, didn't open his eyes.

Eddie would rather have had his friend yell at him. The silence was the worst he had ever experienced. He would have apologized for everything if the words hadn't been stuck in his throat, making the tears fall freely and unjustly with each struggling breath he took. He sat his head back against the wall and closed his eyes, praying to anything that would help ease his suffering. He prayed until he heard movement in front of him, and opening his bloodshot eyes, he saw that Anthony was now standing over him with his hand stretched out "Give me the pistol," he tenderly demanded.

Eddie eyed him, but eventually gave in. He lifted his pant leg and pulled out the small pistol that was always strapped around his ankle, the same pistol he had shot his wife with. He handed it to Anthony, who took it more gently than he had expected.

"You will always be my best friend, Eddie," the tall man with the piercing blue eyes recalled, keeping his gaze on the pistol. "Despite my feelings, I'd still go to hell and back for ya. You were the only family I had."

"Thank you for the eulogy," Eddie commented wearily. "But I'd rather ya just shoot me and get it over with."

Anthony smirked but lightly shook his head. "You're family to me, and I guess as family, I have a duty to make sure ya redeem yourself in times of weakness and hardship."

Eddie sighed, unable to control it. "So what does that mean?"

"It means ya get to face these assholes by yourself." With that, Anthony turned around and walked to the secret door. Eddie watched as he turned the handle and pushed the door open, looking into the speakeasy and hearing the jazz and chatter of the patrons spill into the corridor. Eddie witnessed as Anthony lifted the gun to the ceiling and fired two shots before screaming that a raid was coming up the back entrance. Within seconds, chaos broke out, and Eddie never saw his friend again.

CHAPTER SEVEN

. . . .

Even after Anthony disappeared with the crowds, Eddie could somehow still hear what had erupted on the other side of the threshold, hear the screams and clatter of heels as men and women bolted towards the trap door and main entrance, trying to escape from the invisible authorities. He heard tables and chairs crashing as nothing stood in their way while they stampeded towards safety, fleeing away from the speakeasy.

Everything he had worked for was gone, he knew that now, as he remained seated with his back against the wall. Eddie again closed his eyes and tilted his head back. This was real. Everyone he had cared for and who had cared for him was gone. Most of them permanently, waiting for him at the edge of life, waiting for him to join them. But it wasn't joyous. What waited for him was death in its most common form, revenge in all its purity.

Only if for a night, he told himself as he stood up, *I won't disappoint them*. Eddie took a deep breath, fixed his shirt, and then walked steadily toward the door, wanting to get this over with.

He knew he was still in his speakeasy, but the scene had been drastically altered. Tables and chairs were toppled over, cards and broken glasses thrown about the room, and even the shelf behind the bar was bare, the bottles disappearing down the chute behind the wall. All he could do was put his hands in his pockets and shake his head. Two faulty police raids and the booze still went down the drain. Typical.

Eddie now stood in the middle of the dance floor, the lights all on him. He peered around, staring into the shadows that now surrounded him, pretending to hear the jazz music that had been brutally ended. There were a few dark spots that foretold people were still in the room, but he only stared for a brief moment before looking elsewhere, all his cares leaving him. He just wanted to be done with it.

"Are you not afraid, Mr. Durante?" a deep raspy voice asked ahead of him, his body equally obscured by shadows but unable to hide the large, rough silhouette that stood in front of the booth. He sounded ugly yet respectable, a tough man who didn't mess with anyone unless he was messed with.

Eddie slightly chuckled at him. "What the hell do I have to be afraid of? I'm my biggest enemy."

"No kidding," the voice responded with a light chuckle of its own. "I half hoped you'd be groveling at your feet."

"It's not my style."

"I guess not," the voice responded, and by the way he said it, Eddie swore that if he could see him, he would have watched the man cross his arms and draw in a large breath, an act of slight disappointment in his movements. But he was just a black blob in a shadowed backdrop, so Eddie was left to wonder.

"I'm surprised ya didn't budge when the raid was announced," Eddie commented.

"Please, Mr. Durante," the voice chuckled, somewhat entertained by the comment. "I've spent enough money to keep this joint free of coppers for the evening. I knew no one would be walking through that door except you."

Eddie nodded, his suspicions confirmed.

"I admire you a little, though. Compared to the rest of them, you're quite different," the voice continued out of curiosity. "No cringing, no apologizing. You're taking this like a real man."

Eddie shrugged his shoulders, beyond scared. In fact, he was becoming a little irritated at the pointless conversation. "So are ya going to talk me to death, or what?"

The voice laughed, enjoying the charade. "I'm curious about you. You seem to have no sense of wrong, even for a young man. There's no pain, no remorse," the voice softened into enthusiasm. "No feeling."

Eddie's jaw clenched. The man was fishing, he knew it. He wanted a fight, a little dramatic scene to entertain him, to feel satisfied that he had pushed another man to the edge. Eddie refused to play along. "I'm sorry ya feel that way."

"Strange thing about people when faced with death. Some will do anything to survive, while others just simply look it in the face and accept it. Yet you can't tell who it is until the moment's just right. True colors never come out until the end, when they think there are no second chances." The silhouette shifted and Eddie assumed he was getting comfortable where he was standing. "Take for example your uncle. He was a weeper, melting into a puddle instantly. His bodyguard was no better, except he didn't try to stick around."

Eddie grimaced when he remember the five bullet holes in the man's back.

"Yet, the bootleggers were admirable," the voice

continued. "They embraced their ending. And that torpedo-cousin of yours was just annoying as hell to even watch, so we didn't mess around with him."

Eddie felt heat slipping into his face, his anger surfacing.

"You never know how someone will react when their cornered. You, for instance, embrace your end, unlike your wife—"

"Don't," Eddie spat, before cascading into a soft voice. "Don't talk about my wife."

Suddenly off to the distance, a tap against the floor echoed from some corner, Eddie couldn't tell. It sounded like a cane, and he wondered where it exactly had come from.

"My boss," the husky voice said, replying to the unasked question. "Came to watch the brilliant Eddie Durante die."

Eddie didn't miss the pleasure the man felt when he said the words, and when he felt a creak behind him, he couldn't help but turn to see who it was. All he saw was the dark void where the lights had faded out.

"Of course," the voice contemplated, "there is a slight issue we've had that we need your help with."

Eddie laughed at him. Of course; that's why he was still alive.

"The money, Mr. Durante," the voice persisted, a little more seriously. "As you're probably aware, we found our guns, and plenty of liquor to accommodate our loss. However, it's the money that we can't seem to put our finger on. We'd like to know where it is."

Eddie only smiled. "Go to hell."

It was an answer the man was used to receiving, so he laughed with Eddie out of good humor before responding,

"Maybe you'll tell my boss." Eddie could barely make out the man putting his hand out towards the table in the corner where the white smoke had been, holding it stretched out like an announcer welcoming his next act.

Eddie stared at the black space in the corner, the one with the single trail of smoke that had caught his attention what seemed like hours ago. The lingering smoke was gone now. His ears strained to hear a sound, and when he did, he felt his nerves slightly jump. The sound of a table creaking as someone leaned against it, along with the shuffling of clothing as someone slid out from the booth. The sound of a cane tapping slowly against the floor as the figure walked forward, rhythmically and carefully, dependency evident in the taps.

So he was going to meet the boss. Eddie didn't know if he should feel nervous or proud. It was said that the boss from the Caprice family was an invalid, bed-ridden from some accident, Eddie couldn't remember. Was he really so important that a bed-ridden old fool would come to watch him die? Eddie turned and faced the corner head on. There was no doubt the boss would; the young Durante had done a lot of damage.

Eddie kept his eyes on the corner, the tapping of the cane drawing near to the light. Then, before he knew it, a figure passed the shadow drapes, breaking through the darkness as light spilled across the body. He blinked a couple times, readjusting to the image that was coming towards him. It was a woman dressed in a thick wool coat, wearing a matching-colored cloche hat that was pulled down over the eyes, making it hard for Eddie to see her face. Her actions were fluid yet marked with pain as she leaned in to the cane for support.

Eddie's heart instinctively began to race, pounding in his ears as she drew nearer. The sweat formed on his forehead and palms, the hairs on the back of his neck standing straight up. A coldness had plunged into his body, clawing all the way to his bones, when he saw draped over her shoulder the thick locks of auburn hair.

She stopped near him, leaving almost an arms'-length distance between them. Unbeknownst to him, Eddie was taking hard breaths now, almost gasping as he stared at her. She was the grim reaper to him, and he could almost feel his soul trying to tear away from his body the longer she stood there. As if sensing his vulnerability, the woman reacted in a simple manner. The bell-shaped hat slowly lifted up, exposing the face hidden inside. Past the small brim was a pair of hazel eyes staring up at him in an expression he could not distinguish, because Eddie couldn't get past the recognizable eyes and jagged scars that creased the right side of her face.

"Kate," Eddie whispered, trembling as he spoke the name, feeling his eyes stinging and tears coming to his rescue.

"My boss," the raspy voice said amusingly, a light edge in his tone as he too stepped into the light. "At least, for tonight."

Eddie tore his eyes from her face and took a brief scan of the man he had been previously conversing with, seeing that he was tall and rugged, built like a boxer, with a tailored black suit on. His fedora was pushed back away from his face, revealing his leathered skin, scarred from past fights. There was enjoyment in his light eyes as he pulled out his cigarette case, peeled a cigarette from it, lit it and inhaled deeply. Blowing the smoke out through his nose, he analyzed the cigarette while he addressed Eddie. "I bet you can only imagine what exactly happened that day."

Eddie's eyes went back to Kate, the same lips and soft features meeting him, reminding him just how real she had once been, how much he still wanted her. But the expression she wore was something she had never worn before; it was a new expression formed from tragedy and betrayal and something entirely different.

"Would you like to explain it to him, Mrs. Durante?" the man asked, taking another puff from his cigarette.

Kate's eyes were unwavering when she said yes.

To Eddie, despite hearing so little, found that her voice hadn't changed. It was still soft and tender, beautiful in its tone. But behind the lyrical exterior was an animosity that crept up on the listeners as she spoke, leaving a bittersweet feeling that made him cringe.

"The only explanation there is," she addressed to Eddie, "was that I was just too terrified to die. You already know half the story, with the men being shot, me being shot." He saw her lips quiver as she remembered, her story becoming more descriptive as she told him. "Max's neck wound, his blood in between my fingers as I tried to steer that car. I didn't realize we had reached the docks until I saw the water coming towards the windshield."

Eddie's frame began to shake as he tried to breath, remembering the day just as vividly as she had. He blinked a couple times, trying to see through his increasingly blurry vision.

"I threw myself into the backseat when I saw the water. It wasn't me who went through the windshield. It was Max." Kate looked at the ground, as if finding her composure there. Regaining it, she lifted her gaze back to her husband. "That's how he died, Eddie. He had been alive until that point. He was stuck in the windshield when the water started coming in, the coldest water I've ever felt, and with all the strength I had, I grabbed Max by his clothes and pulled him out. There wasn't much air left in the cab by the time I was able to move him, but

I took my last deep breath, and I swam through that opening he had created. I was in so much pain though that it was hard to swim, and the jagged glass scrapped against my dress, along with my face." To prove her point, Kate pushed the brim of her hat back to reveal three jagged scars, barely missing her eye.

"I pushed myself as hard as I could towards the surface, losing air as I went because I just couldn't hold it in anymore. Before I gulped in the water, I broke through the surface and breathed in until my lungs couldn't take it. The water was freezing, so cold it almost burned like fire. I tried to keep swimming but I couldn't move my legs anymore, so I floated on my back, trying to use my arms instead. I felt so tired, and all I could think of was sleeping. Then after what felt like a lifetime, I heard shouting, and then some men pulling me onto a small boat. I don't remember them asking questions, just trying to keep me awake as they took me to the hospital. Everyone kept asking my name, but I couldn't tell them. I knew you'd come back."

A tear helplessly fell down Eddie's cheek as he stared at his wife, both of them knowing that he had gone back. He had searched for her to make sure she hadn't survived. Eddie wanted nothing more than to beg for forgiveness, but he knew it would be pointless.

The man, who had been smoking and enjoying the story, continued the story when Kate couldn't. "The coppers went searching the hospitals before you did. One of our paid informants found her, heard how she had gotten there from one of the doctors, and when he spoke to her, Mrs. Durante said that she wanted to speak to one of us. He informed us of her request, and we made sure her identity was concealed in order to protect her. I went personally to hear what she had to say, and that's when this," he extended his hands in awe, a smile of satisfaction on his face. "This all came to being."

Eddie stole a glance at him before returning it to Kate. He understood what had happened. It was exactly what Anthony had expected; revenge in its purist form.

Kate shifted, the pain evident from her grimace and the way she favored her leg. Eddie's impulse as a husband was to help her, but he stopped himself when the man walked up to them, standing right behind Kate. "The whereabouts of the money, Mr. Durante."

"What happens afterwards, once you get what you want?" Eddie demanded, blind fury overtaking his reasoning. "Because if you hurt my wife in any way —"

The man smiled to the point of laughter. "Take a look at her, Mr. Durante. I ain't the one who hurt her. And remember, on this plan, she's my boss."

Eddie recoiled at the thought. They had planned each other's murders.

Without a word, Kate stretched her hand out, asking for only one item. Eddie looked at her hand and then at her, somewhat confused until he realized that he only had one thing left on him. Slowly, he put his hand in his pocket and drew out the magnetic key. He looked at the key, having a hard time believing it all as he gave it to her.

Key in hand, Kate walked unsteadily towards the bar, the two men watching as she moved to the wall that was next to the shelves where the liquor had been stacked, the decorative paneling and the designed holes matching the other walls. Sticking the key into one of the holes, she heard it unlatch, and then opened one of the panels to reveal a small door that was chest high. Inside was a small safe, and already knowing the combination, Kate unlocked it and took out a black bag. Closing the safe and the door, she limped back with the bag in hand.

Eddie watched her in amazement. She had known the whole time. She had watched him, her smoke lingering from the corner of the room, knowing everything that had gone on. He had felt her eyes on him, but he had never known it was actually her.

Kate approached the man, handing him the bag. She didn't linger to see if her guess was correct, but Eddie saw that the man was satisfied once he looked inside and his face lit up. However, his gaze on the man was equally short, for Kate approached him and handed the key back. Eddie slowly reached out to take it, wondering why she was still here if she had known.

Eddie found his answer when he saw the way her gaze fell on him, a gleaming affection that she couldn't secure. Subconscious or not, it had survived through everything. Eddie couldn't help but reach out and caress her cheek with his fingertips, feeling the raised imprint of the scars. He held back a choke as he whispered, "I'm so sorry, baby."

Kate, who could have reacted in so many ways, simply tilted her head as she held her hand against his, and keeping his touch within reach, she turned her head to kiss his palm. He could swear that a million shock waves hit his body when she kissed him, and he trembled from the impact. He couldn't take his eyes from her, and when she finally looked back at him, his ears chased after every word she spoke. "Not as much as I am," she replied, her own eyes sparkling with remorse.

Before he knew it, Kate had moved by him and was walking towards the entrance door of the speakeasy. He watched her as she disappeared into the shadows, the tapping of the cane still echoing off the floors until the creaking of the entrance door as it was pulled open overpowered it. At that point, he could make out her silhouette against the trail of light bulbs that hung overhead. He couldn't take his eyes away, seeing for the first time how alike he and his wife were.

Eddie was so lost in his observation that it blinded him when the first swing of the baseball bat smashed into his body. There was no point to see how many of them were surrounding him, but even as he was beaten down to his knees and then to the floor, he couldn't take his gaze from the distancing silhouette. He groaned from the pain as the men beat him, his bones cracking and breaking under his skin while his blood began to spill out of the wounds. But as the baseball bats continued to crash down on him, and even when one of his eyes failed to see again, Eddie kept his attention only on his wife.

In the moments before the end came, Eddie felt his heartbeats begin to distance themselves and grow further apart with each passing promise he made to himself:

I will hold her again, kiss her again, feel everything about her.
We will spend every moment making it up to ourselves.
We will love each other the way we were meant to.

Eddie smiled now, swearing that he could feel his soul drifting after her.

Kate, he thought in his finale, *see you in hell, sweetheart.*

ACKNOWLEDGMENTS

. . . .

I'm very grateful to my family, friends, coworkers, and acquaintances that have supported me and my writing throughout the years. Thank you so much for the love, support and encouragement that all of you have given me. I appreciate it beyond words.

Regarding this novella, I have to give a special thank you to four people who really helped it along. A very special thank you to Gina and my mom, for being both my editors and cheerleaders; to Alex, who helped me research aspects of the story when I was at a loss; and to Dean, who created the breathless cover that I never thought was possible.

With all my heart, thank you.

A. M. Dunnewin grew up with a taste for mysteries and thrillers, inherited ever so lovingly from her family. With a B.A. in Psychology, she's a gambler of words, obsessed with chai tea, and addicted to books—everything from classical literature to graphic novels. Her other hobbies include art, history, music, and watching classic films. She currently dwells in Northern California.

For more information, visit amdunnewin.com, or find her across social media on Facebook, Twitter, Instagram, or Pinterest.

www.ingramcontent.com/pod-product-compliance
Lightning Source LLC
Chambersburg PA
CBHW020622120726
47905CB00003B/906